A book
is a present you can open
again and again.

THIS BOOK BELONGS TO

FROM

Goldilocks and the Three Bears

Adapted from an English folk tale

General Editor
Bernice E. Cullinan
New York University

Retold by
Seva Spanos

Illustrated by
Chi Chung

World Book, Inc.
a Scott Fetzer company
Chicago London Sydney Toronto

Printed in the United States of America
ISBN 0-7166-1603-3
Library of Congress Catalog Card No. 91-65467
5 6 7 8 9 10 11 12 13 14 15 99 98 97 96 95 94

Cover design by Rosa Cabrera
Book design by PROVIZION

ONCE UPON A TIME, there were three bears who lived in a house in the forest. Papa Bear was a great big bear with a great big booming voice. Mama Bear was a middle-sized bear with a mild, middle-sized voice. And Baby Bear was a wee little bear with a wee little whispering voice. Together, they were a very interesting family to talk to.

ONE MORNING, the three bears cooked a hot cereal called porridge for their breakfast. When they sat down to eat, Papa Bear boomed in his great big voice, "My porridge is too hot!"

Mama Bear agreed. In her middle-sized voice, she mildly said, "My porridge is too hot."

Then Baby Bear whispered in his wee little voice, "My porridge is too hot too!"

So the three bears put their heads together and tried to figure out what to do. Then they knew. They would go exploring in the forest until their porridge had cooled off. As the three bears walked, they sang their favorite song.

To see in the forest, 6 eyes have we:
2 big, 2 middle, 2 little.
We're just as fit as a fiddle
To walk in the forest and see.
Six eyes can really see—
Yes! Six eyes can really see.

To hear in the forest, 6 ears have we:
2 big, 2 middle, 2 little.
We're just as fit as a fiddle
To walk in the forest and hear.
Six ears can really hear—
Yes! Six ears can really hear.

To sniff in the forest, 3 snouts have we:
1 big, 1 middle, 1 little.
We're just as fit as a fiddle
To walk in the forest and sniff.
Three snouts can really sniff—
Yes! Three snouts can really sniff.

When all is said and done,
Three bears are better than one—
Yes! Three bears are better than one!

THAT MORNING, the three bears looked with their eyes, listened with their ears, and sniffed with their snouts as they explored the forest.

WHILE the three bears were away, a little girl named Goldilocks came walking by their house. Goldilocks was very curious to know who lived in that house. So she walked up to the door. She knocked and listened, but no one answered. She knocked again and listened. Still no one answered.

Then Goldilocks saw that a window was open. She decided to do some exploring. She walked to the window, stood on her tiptoes, and peeked in.

GOLDILOCKS saw a kitchen with a table set for three. On the table were three bowls of porridge: a great big bowl, a middle-sized bowl, and a wee little bowl.

Goldilocks sniffed the porridge. It smelled so good that she got very hungry.

Then Goldilocks thought, "I can't stop exploring now, just when I've found something good to eat!" So she decided to climb through the window and into the kitchen to taste the porridge.

FIRST, Goldilocks tasted Papa Bear's great big bowl of porridge. "Oh, my, this is too hot!" she said, dropping the spoon on the table.

Then Goldilocks tasted Mama Bear's middle-sized bowl of porridge. "Oh, no, this is too cold!" she said, pushing the bowl away.

Finally, Goldilocks tasted Baby Bear's wee little bowl of porridge. "Oh, yes," she said, "this is just right!" And Goldilocks ate Baby Bear's porridge until it was all gone.

THEN Goldilocks thought, "I wonder what else I might find in this house." And she went through the door that led to the living room. There she saw three chairs: a great big chair, a middle-sized chair, and a wee little chair.

Seeing the chairs made Goldilocks feel very tired. So she decided to sit down for a while.

FIRST, Goldilocks sat on Papa Bear's great big chair. "Oh, my, this is too high!" she said as she knocked its cushion to the floor.

Then Goldilocks sat on Mama Bear's middle-sized chair. "Oh, no, this is too low!" she said as she sank deep into its center.

Finally, Goldilocks sat on Baby Bear's wee little chair. "Oh, yes," she said, "this is just right!" And Goldilocks rocked and she rocked and she rocked till the chair broke.

THEN Goldilocks thought, "I wonder if I can find someplace else to rest in this house." And she went through the door that led to the bedroom. There she saw three beds: a great big bed, a middle-sized bed, and a wee little bed.

Seeing the beds made Goldilocks feel very sleepy. So she decided to lie down for a while.

FIRST, Goldilocks tried Papa Bear's great big bed. "Oh, my, this is too hard!" she said, mussing up the covers.

Then Goldilocks tried Mama Bear's middle-sized bed. "Oh, no, this is too soft!" she said, squashing the pillow.

Finally, Goldilocks tried Baby Bear's wee little bed. "Oh, yes," she said, "this is just right!" And Goldilocks fell fast asleep.

SOON the three bears returned from the forest and walked into their kitchen. First, Papa Bear saw his spoon on the table. In his great big voice, he boomed, "Someone has been eating my porridge!"

Then Mama Bear saw that her bowl was out of place. In her middle-sized voice, she mildly said, "Someone has been eating my porridge."

Finally, Baby Bear saw his empty bowl. In his wee little voice, he whispered, "Someone has been eating my porridge and has eaten it all up!"

With their eyes, the three bears looked at their porridge. Next, they listened closely with their ears. Then they lifted their snouts into the air and sniffed. At last, they put their heads together and tried to figure out what had happened. Then they knew. Someone had come exploring in their kitchen and had eaten their food.

"Yes," the three bears said, "there's no doubt about it."

NEXT, the three bears walked into their living room. First, Papa Bear saw his cushion on the floor. In his great big voice, he boomed, "Someone has been sitting in my chair!"

Then Mama Bear saw her chair sunk deep in the center. In her middle-sized voice, she mildly said, "Someone has been sitting in my chair."

Finally, Baby Bear saw that his chair was broken. In his wee little voice, he whispered, "Someone has been sitting in my chair and has broken it!"

With their eyes, the three bears looked at their chairs. Next, they listened closely with their ears. Then they lifted their snouts into the air and sniffed. At last, they put their heads together and tried to figure out what had happened. Then they knew. Someone had come exploring in their living room and had sat on their chairs.

"Yes," the three bears said, "there's no doubt about it."

AT LAST, the three bears walked into their bedroom. First, Papa Bear saw the mussed-up covers on his bed. In his great big voice, he boomed, "Someone has been lying on my bed!"

Then Mama Bear saw her squashed pillow. In her middle-sized voice, she mildly said, "Someone has been lying on my bed."

Finally, Baby Bear saw his bed. In his wee little voice, he whispered, "Someone has been lying on my bed. And there she is!"

With their eyes, the three bears looked at Goldilocks. Next, they listened closely with their ears. Then they lifted their snouts into the air and sniffed. At last, they put their heads together and tried to figure out who this someone was. Then they knew. This was the someone who had eaten their porridge and sat on their chairs. And here she was, fast asleep!

"Yes," the three bears said, "there's no doubt about it."

JUST THEN, Goldilocks woke up. When she saw the three bears, she leapt up and ran home as fast as her legs could carry her.

"OH, MY," Papa Bear boomed, "I think we frightened that little girl!"

"Oh, no," Mama Bear said mildly, "do you think she was afraid of us?"

"Oh, yes," Baby Bear whispered, "there's no doubt about it!"

AND Baby Bear was right, because Goldilocks never went exploring all by herself again.

To Parents

Children delight in hearing and reading folk tales. *Goldilocks and the Three Bears* will provide your child with an entertaining story as well as a bridge into learning some important concepts. Here are a few easy and natural ways your child can express feelings and understandings about the story. You know your child and can best judge which ideas will be the most enjoyable.

Involve your child while reading the story. Use different voices, and encourage your child to play one part. A variation is to read just the narrative, and have your child say all the speaking parts.

Enjoy the bears' walking song. Take turns pointing to the bears' eyes, ears, snouts, and heads. Ask your child questions such as, "What do the bears do with their eyes?" "How do the bears hear?" "What do the bears sniff with?" "Can you point to your eyes? ears? nose? head?" "What do you use them for?"

Recite the three bears' song with your child. Use motions for *walk, see, hear,* and *sniff.* Perform the song for any willing listener.

As you read the sentences about the bears' porridge, chairs, and beds, ask your child to act out what Goldilocks did with each one.

Draw lines to divide a large sheet of paper into four parts. Work with your child to draw pictures of the four things in the story that come in sets of three: bears, bowls, chairs, and beds.

Ask your child to tell you what these things are like: the bowls of porridge (too hot, too cold, just right), the chairs (too high, too low, just right), and the beds (too hard, too soft, just right). Ask questions such as, "Which is the biggest bowl of porridge?" and "Which chair is the littlest?"